Princess Miranda was tired
of being a princess.

3

She was tired of dressing up. She was sick of crowns and jewels.

"You have to wear them," said the queen, "because you're a princess." "They give me such a headache," Miranda complained.

One day she went to her godmother, who was a witch. "Turn me into something different," she begged.

So Miranda's godmother turned
her into a frog.

Miranda liked being a frog. She liked floating on lily pads ...

... and leaping through the leaves.

And catching flies!

One evening she leapt into a park where a young gardener was working.

"Look at that frog!" the gardener said to his friend. "Let's catch it and keep it in the lily pond."

Next morning, the gardener
came to look at his very own frog.
Miranda was leaping around.

The gardener laughed.

"If I found a girl as funny as you,
I might even marry her." he joked.

"Take me home," croaked Miranda.
"A frog that speaks?" said the
gardener, surprised.

So the gardener took Miranda
back to his cottage, and she sat
beside him in a bowl.

"If you give me a kiss," said Miranda, "I might even turn into a princess!"

"I don't kiss frogs," said the gardener, but he did it anyway. Suddenly a pretty girl stood beside him. He fell deeply in love.

17

"Princess Frog, will you marry me?" he said.

But Miranda wasn't quite sure.

"No more dressing up?" she asked,

The gardener laughed.

"Jeans and T-shirt for you, my love."

"No more crowns," said Miranda.

"They give me such a headache."

The gardener laughed.

"No crowns here," he said.

"And I'll need to keep leaping," Miranda added.

"I'll build you a trampoline," promised the gardener.

"Ok," said Miranda, "If I don't have to dress like a princess, I will marry you."

And so they were married,
though the queen did NOT
approve of Miranda's
wedding outfit!

And of course they lived happily
ever after.

But every once in a while, Miranda
slipped back into her frog skin
and floated happily on a lily pad
in the pond.

28

Puzzle 1

Put these pictures in the correct order.
Which event do you think is most important?
Now try writing the story in your own words!

Puzzle 2

Choose the correct speech bubbles for each character. Can you think of any others? Turn over to find the answers.

Answers

Puzzle 1

The correct order is: 1e, 2b, 3d, 4f, 5c, 6a.

Puzzle 2

The frog/princess: 1, 4

The gardener: 2, 3

The queen: 5, 6

Look out for more Hopscotch Twisty Tales and Fairy Tales:

TWISTY TALES

The Princess and the Frozen Peas
ISBN 978 1 4451 0669 4*
ISBN 978 1 4451 0675 5

Snow White Sees the Light
ISBN 978 1 4451 0670 0*
ISBN 978 1 4451 0676 2

The Elves and the Trendy Shoes
ISBN 978 1 4451 0672 4*
ISBN 978 1 4451 0678 6

The Three Frilly Goats Fluff
ISBN 978 1 4451 0671 7*
ISBN 978 1 4451 0677 9

Princess Frog
ISBN 978 1 4451 0673 1*
ISBN 978 1 4451 0679 3

Rumpled Stilton Skin
ISBN 978 1 4451 0674 8*
ISBN 978 1 4451 0680 9

Jack and the Bean Pie
ISBN 978 1 4451 0182 8

Brownilocks and the Three Bowls of Cornflakes
ISBN 978 1 4451 0183 5

Cinderella's Big Foot
ISBN 978 1 4451 0184 2

Little Bad Riding Hood
ISBN 978 1 4451 0185 9

Sleeping Beauty – 100 Years Later
ISBN 978 1 4451 0186 6

FAIRY TALES

The Three Little Pigs
ISBN 978 0 7496 7905 7

Little Red Riding Hood
ISBN 978 0 7496 7907 1

Goldilocks and the Three Bears
ISBN 978 0 7496 7903 3

Hansel and Gretel
ISBN 978 0 7496 7904 0

Rapunzel
ISBN 978 0 7496 7906 4

Rumpelstiltskin
ISBN 978 0 7496 7908 8

The Elves and the Shoemaker
ISBN 978 0 7496 8543 0

The Ugly Duckling
ISBN 978 0 7496 8544 7

Sleeping Beauty
ISBN 978 0 7496 8545 4

The Frog Prince
ISBN 978 0 7496 8546 1

The Princess and the Pea
ISBN 978 0 7496 8547 8

Dick Whittington
ISBN 978 0 7496 8548 5

Cinderella
ISBN 978 0 7496 7417 5

Snow White and the Seven Dwarfs
ISBN 978 0 7496 7418 2

The Pied Piper of Hamelin
ISBN 978 0 7496 7419 9

Jack and the Beanstalk
ISBN 978 0 7496 7422 9

The Three Billy Goats Gruff
ISBN 978 0 7496 7420 5

For more Hopscotch books go to:
www.franklinwatts.co.uk

*hardback